Lesley Wright Rathbone

Illustrated by Aldila Permata

Alice's Wish and a Magic Fish

Pegasus

A CIP catalogue record for this title is
available from the British Library.
ISBN 978-1-80468-013-1

PEGASUS is an imprint of Pegasus Elliot
MacKenzie Publishers Ltd.
www.pegasuspublishers.com

First Published in 2023

PEGASUS
Sheraton House Castle
Park Cambridge England

Printed & Bound in Great Britain

Dedication

To Joseph - my intrepid little traveller. I can't

wait to show you all of these places.

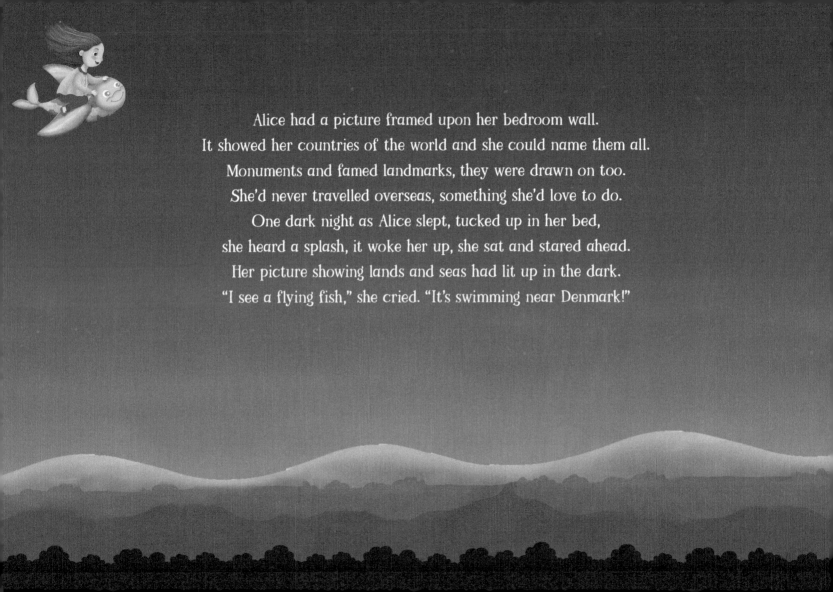

Alice had a picture framed upon her bedroom wall.
It showed her countries of the world and she could name them all.
Monuments and famed landmarks, they were drawn on too.
She'd never travelled overseas, something she'd love to do.
One dark night as Alice slept, tucked up in her bed,
she heard a splash, it woke her up, she sat and stared ahead.
Her picture showing lands and seas had lit up in the dark.
"I see a flying fish," she cried. "It's swimming near Denmark!"

This magic fish had rainbow scales, he gave a little wave.
"Hello," he said. "My name is Finn." He seemed quite well behaved.
He winked and jumped out of the frame, he landed with a flip.
"I know you long to see the world, I'll take you on a trip."

Alice beamed, jumped on his back, ready for the flight.

They flew downstairs and out the door while Alice held on tight.

"There's so much we will see," said Finn. "Now ready, set, let's go."

They zoomed past clouds, the moon and stars, the street lamps down below.

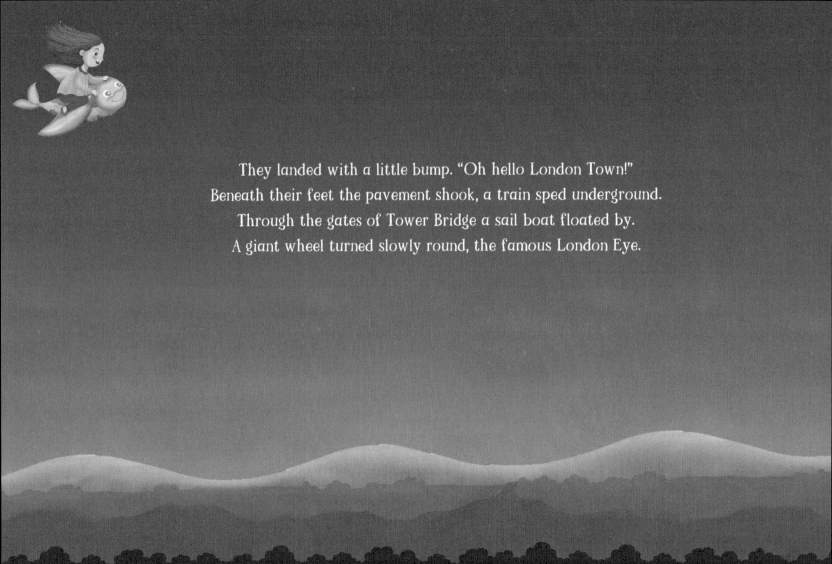

They landed with a little bump. "Oh hello London Town!"
Beneath their feet the pavement shook, a train sped underground.
Through the gates of Tower Bridge a sail boat floated by.
A giant wheel turned slowly round, the famous London Eye.

A zoo, museums, Big Ben too! They peered in restaurants
and ran through London Dungeon's vaults where zombies love to haunt.
"What a super place," said Finn. "But time for us to go."
They zoomed past clouds, the moon and stars, the street lamps down below.

They landed with a gentle bump. "Bonsoir," laughed Finn and Alice.
Cobbled streets and winding lanes, it seemed they'd flown to Paris.
They danced along the rain-washed streets and skipped back up again.
Past monuments, the Notre Dame, the glistening River Seine.

Alice tried a warm croissant and cakes with pink iced flowers.
Whilst in the distance, brightly lit, there stood the Eiffel Tower.
"What a lovely place," said Finn. "But time for us to go."
They zoomed past clouds, the moon and stars, the street lamps down below.

They landed with a bump again, Alice felt quite dizzy.
People rushing to and fro. "Well this is New York City!"
Yellow taxis, beeping horns and street food everywhere.
Shops and theatres, high rise towers, the bright lights of Times Square.

One tall building stretching high, its name the Empire State.
A sheet of ice in Central Park where people love to skate.
"What a busy place," said Finn. "But time for us to go."
They zoomed past clouds, the moon and stars, the street lamps down below.

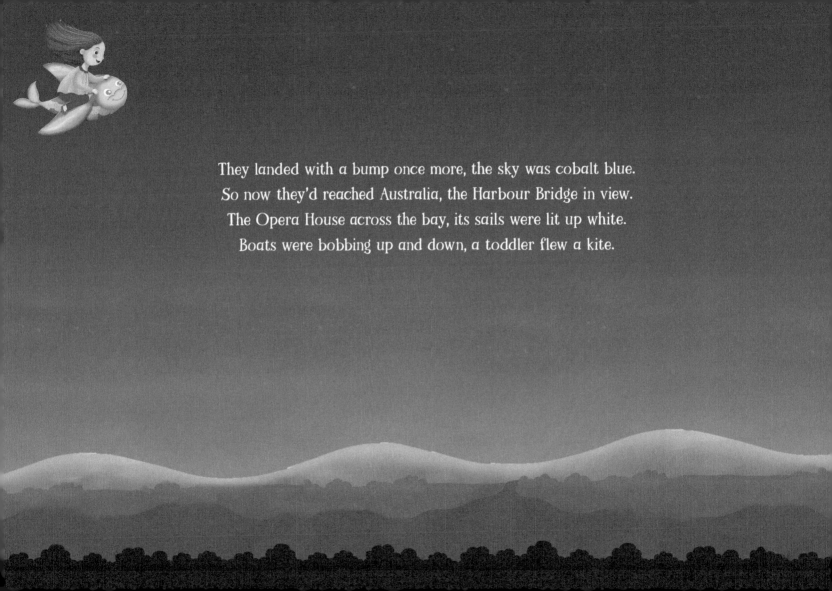

They landed with a bump once more, the sky was cobalt blue.
So now they'd reached Australia, the Harbour Bridge in view.
The Opera House across the bay, its sails were lit up white.
Boats were bobbing up and down, a toddler flew a kite.

They travelled through the bush and saw koala bears and snakes.
Emus, possums, kangaroos and bugs of different shapes.
"What an awesome place," said Finn. "But time to get you home."
Alice felt so sad to leave the places she'd been shown.

She crept into her darkened house and tiptoed up the stairs.

She climbed beneath her soft warm sheets, hugging her stuffed bears.

Her fleeting trip around the globe had been a dream come true.

And even though she felt so tired her heart was happy too.

"I'd better get to sleep," she thought, as soon the sun would rise.

She looked up at her wall again before she closed her eyes.

Her picture was aglow once more and Finn was back in view.
He gave a wave, a wink, a smile, then dived into the blue.

About the Author

Lesley has always loved writing stories and poems. She wrote her first poem about the January sales aged nine. Since then Lesley has studied feature writing and has previously written for newspapers and magazines. The inspiration for this story came from a map of the world which hangs on her son's bedroom wall. Lesley works in television and lives in London with her husband and young son.

Alice's Wish And A Magic Fish is her first book.